To Lori and Yvette, because without you, you, you, there would be no Me, Me, Me — A.D.

To Annika for creating these adorable girls, Yvette for bringing them into my life and Ila for helping me bring them to life — L.J.S.

The snacks in this story are

chocolatines (shock-oh-lah-teen): French sweet pastry rolls with a piece or two of chocolate in the center

pepparkakor (pehp-pahr-kah-koor): traditional Swedish ginger cookies

saft (suhft): a Swedish drink, usually made with berries

Text © 2017 Annika Dunklee
Illustrations © 2017 Lori Joy Smith

Kids Can Press gratefully acknowledges the financial support of the Government of Ontario, through the Ontario Media Development Corporation; the Ontario Arts Council; the Canada Council for the Arts; and the Government of Canada, through the CBF, for our publishing activity.

Published in Canada and the U.S. by Kids Can Press Ltd.
25 Dockside Drive, Toronto, ON M5A 0B5

Kids Can Press is a Corus Entertainment Inc. company

www.kidscanpress.com

The artwork in this book was rendered digitally.
The text is set in Garamond and Clue.

Edited by Yvette Ghione
Designed by Michael Reis

Printed and bound in Shenzhen, China, in 3/2017 by C&C Offset

CM 17 0 9 8 7 6 5 4 3 2 1

Library and Archives Canada Cataloguing in Publication

Dunklee, Annika, 1965–, author
      Me, me, me / written by Annika Dunklee ; illustrated by
Lori Joy Smith.

ISBN 978-1-77138-660-9 (hardback)

      I. Smith, Lori Joy, 1973–, illustrator II. Title.

PS8607.U542M39 2017   jC813'.6   C2016-906804-8

Me, Me, Me

Written by Annika Dunklee

Illustrated by Lori Joy Smith

Kids Can Press

This is Annie, Lillemor and Lilianne. They are best friends for many reasons. Speaking another language is just one of them.

(Even though Annie made hers up, she is pretty sure it still counts.)

* For sure!
* Of course!
* You betcha!

They all get along very well together …
Usually, that is.

One day, their teacher announced that there was going to be a school talent show. Annie could hardly contain herself.

I know! Let's enter the talent show as an all-girl singing group!

Lillemor and Lilianne really liked this idea.

Vad kul!*

Génial!*

* What fun!   * Brilliant!

The three girls decided to hold a meeting to talk about it further.

Like any successful meeting, snacks were essential. Lillemor brought *saft* and *pepparkakor*.

Lilianne brought *chocolatines*, and Annie brought
cheese-and-pickle sandwiches.

Order of Business #1

First, they had to choose the song they would sing.

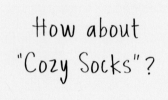

How about
"Cozy Socks"?

Oh, I LOVE
that song!

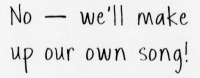

No — we'll make
up our own song!

Lillemor and Lilianne shrugged.

Order of Business #2

Next, they needed to decide on their costumes.

Order of Business #3

They also had to pick their roles in the group.

I should definitely be the lead singer.

Why do you get to decide ... again?

I told you — because it was *my* idea.

Lillemor and Lilianne looked at each other
and rolled their eyes.

Order of Business #4

Last, the three girls needed to come up with a name for their group.

How about **Tre Vänner?**＊

I don't like the sound of that one. Next!

Les Trois Amies?＊

Nope. Not that one, either.

＊ Three Friends

＊ The Three Friends

Lillemor and Lilianne didn't know what to say.

I'll think up a really good name while I warm up my voice.

Do Re Mi Fa So La Ti ...
Do Re Mi ... Mi, Mi, Mi ... Mi

I've got it! We'll enter the talent show as the **Mi Mi Mis!**

!

!

Lillemor and Lilianne couldn't believe their ears.

Annie took a moment to think about this.

Over the weekend, Annie practiced her made-up song all by herself.

But something was missing. So Annie decided to ask two other girls from class, Penny and Ella, to join her.

Penny and Ella looked at each other and burst out laughing.

Things weren't quite working out as Annie had planned …

Meanwhile, Lillemor and Lilianne
practiced singing their song as a duet.

But something was missing.

So Lillemor and Lilianne chose a different song instead.
One without high notes.

That night, Annie thought about the talent show
and the Snowflakes and Lillemor and Lilianne.
She knew what she had to do.

On Monday, Annie met Lillemor and Lilianne at school like she always did. Unlike other mornings, however, no one said a word. It was very awkward. Until finally …

Lillemor and Lilianne sighed with relief.

The next day, the girls held another meeting.

Order of Business #1

This time they *all* decided on the song they would sing.

Order of Business #2

They decided they would *all* take a turn singing the lead part.

Order of Business #3

They decided they would *all* wear dresses … in sparkling silver!

Order of Business #4

They *all* decided on the perfect name for their new group. They took the first letter from each of their names – A-L-L – and came up with …

☆ ALL ONE! ☆

And when Annie, Lillemor and Lilianne entered the talent show as All One …